IN CTHULHU WE TRUST

The Collected Advice Columns of **Dear Cthulhu**

Vol. 8

PATRICK THOMAS

PADWOLF
PUBLISHING

PADWOLF PUBLISHING INC.
WWW.PADWOLF.COM
www.facebook.com/Padwolf

WWW.PATTHOMAS.NET
WWW.DEARCTHULHU.COM

www.facebook.com/PatrickThomasAuthor

I_PatrickThomas @ Twitter

IN CTHULHU WE TRUST
The Collected Advice Columns of Dear Cthulhu Vol. 8

© 2025 Patrick Thomas

This is the first time these letters have been in print form.

Book edited by John L. French

Cover Art and Design by Patrick Thomas

Dear Cthulhu is © & TM Patrick Thomas

ISBN 13 digit 978-1-958310-11-3
First printing. Printed in the USA

If you have any additional questions that Cthulhu can answer, and Cthulhu can answer all questions, Dear Cthulhu welcomes letters and questions at DearCthulhu@ dearcthulhu.com. All letters become the property of Dear Cthulhu and may be used in future columns. Sending financial offerings along with your questions is not necessary but is always appreciated.

**Anyone foolish enough to follow Dear Cthulhu's advice
does so at their own peril.**

To All who have supported the Dear Cthulhu Empire across magazines, books, on the radio, and in their hearts.

Cthulhu acknowledges that you are more intellegent, wise, and attractive than the rest of your human ilk.

Be grateful.

*Cthulhu will one day rise up
to claim the Earth and its inhabitants as his own.
The Great Old One has looked
upon Humankind and found it lacking.
Cthulhu has deemed it necessary
to prepare Humankind for his coming
Thus, Cthulhu now answers humanity's questions
to help them better themselves
to one day better serve him.*

Dear Cthulhu,

I am not very good at interacting with people, particularly female–type people. They bring out all sorts of feelings and thoughts that make me stop being able to act normally. I never know how to talk to them. Or anyone, for that matter. The few times I've tried to make conversation with a woman I found attractive, they have been… rather unkind.

I code software for a living. You'd think I'd be able to do that from home so I wouldn't have to interact with anybody, but the company I work for insists on us coming in one day a week. It claims it helps with team building and camaraderie. They pay more and have better benefits than the only other job I've ever had, so I go along with it. Honestly, it's kind of nice to be around other people who speak to me. Sure, it's only about work-related things, but I get lonely so I'll take what I can get.

Which leads me to my problem. I live in a major metropolitan area and don't have a car, so I have to commute on the subway. I don't know if you've ever had the experience, but it tends to be cramped and overcrowded. Finding a seat during rush hour is akin to winning the lottery. Most people have to stand.

One fateful day, one of the lines on my route was down, so my train had to pick up the slack. We were packed in even tighter than usual. I always try to be respectful and leave at least a couple inches between me and the next person, but it was impossible that day. I ended up standing behind a beautiful woman who might've been described in decades past as bootylicious. We made a sudden stop in the tunnel, which ended up throwing her backside up against my lower front, if you get my drift. Oddly enough, she didn't try to move away and just sort of snuggled in against me.

I didn't move either, because it was the closest I'd ever been to a woman. It was magical and part of me reacted. It felt so good I didn't want to or dare move. I was prepared to stay on that train all day if she did. Bootylicious must have noticed my sudden growth because she turned her neck to look me in the eyes. She smiled, licked her lips, and gave me a wink. Before I realized what was happening, she was rubbing, then grinding her caboose up and down along my train track. I'd like to say I was working on that railroad all the live long day but maybe thirty seconds later my steam whistle blew. All my pent-up anxiety and more exited my body in a way I had never experienced before. At least, not with a partner.

I must have moaned or something because she turned back again, gazed from my eyes to my groin, then bit her bottom lip. The train came to a stop. She blew me a kiss and got off. Me, I'd gotten off between stops.

If I had to describe how I was feeling, it was a mixture of happy, relaxed, and more contented than I'd ever been. I spent the entire day at work with a glorious smile plastered across my face that just wouldn't go away. I talked with my co-workers without even thinking about it.

I looked for her on the ride home. I didn't see her, despite riding back and forth on my line until dark. The next morning, I got up early and rode the subway to work, even though I didn't have to be there. I maneuvered my way through the crowd on the train, searching for Bootylicious. I spotted her getting on in the third car and made a note of her stop. Her eyes met mine and Bootylicious maneuvered so she was in front of me in the same position as yesterday, despite the train not being crowded and a couple seats being open. She pressed up against me and did more of the same. And by more, I mean it. Bootylicious rubbed against me, then flexed her gluteus maximuses (maximi?) hard enough to crack walnuts. I lasted almost a minute that time. Standing stunned in the afterglow, I felt I should say something to her, words equal parts romantic and grateful that would express the depths of my emotions and melt her heart. I held back the first thing that came to mind. It would be creepy to ask her to marry me. Before I could think of a replacement line, she leaned her whole body up against mine and stayed there like we were a couple. Speaking would break whatever spell was happening, so I basked in her nearness. Her hair smelled like lavender.

When we got to what I assumed was her work stop, she pulled away and again blew me a kiss. I rode a few more stops to a station I knew I could cross over at and headed home. The next morning I left early and got off at her station, then waited on the platform until I saw her.

Bootylicious acted like she didn't know me, which admittedly hurt my feelings. We stood apart until the train arrived. Booty got on first before, winking at me before she went through the doors. She took up her position first and I joined her.

As the door shut, she pressed up against me. This time I lasted almost until her stop.

This went on for months. After each time, I felt like I should speak to her, but the moment never seemed right, and whatever words I thought of or prepared seemed woefully inadequate.

When I finally got up the nerve to say something, I barely got two words out before she put her finger over my lips and said, "Shush. Don't."

It was then that I realized that she was the perfect woman. At least for me. On our six-month anniversary, I wanted to get her a gift of some sort, but wasn't sure what would be appropriate. After all, other than being utterly certain that she was my perfect woman, I knew nothing about her, not even her name. Unless by some bizarre twist of the universe, it was Bootylicious.

Not knowing about her life proved to be my undoing that very day.

I got to her platform early. The plan was, as always, we'd pretend not to know each other, but this time she wasn't alone. Some guy was with *my* woman! While this loser had his nose buried in his phone, Bootylicious broke from tradition and met my eyes. She shook her head and pointed to the ring on her left hand, then to the loser. To be honest, I'd never noticed the ring before. My heart seemed to drop into my gut and I had to force myself from vomiting. My precious Bootylicious was married!?

How could Booty betray me like this? How'd she expect me to react to this revelation? To her betrayal of me, of us? How could she bring another man to our most intimate of places? I didn't know how to react either. I was jealous as hell and wanted to punch this guy, as long as I didn't have to talk to him before or after.

Booty tried to motion me to not get on the train. I ignored

her and stepped on behind the two of them. For the first time in half a year, I stood on the morning train alone. I was hoping he'd get off at an earlier stop, but she got off first after giving him a kiss on the lips, which made me furious. Despite all of our intimacy, I'd never gotten a kiss.

I followed loser boy to see where he got off, but stopped short of following him off of the train.

The rest of my day was utter turmoil. Ultimately, I came to the conclusion that her being married didn't really change anything between us. Things could go on the way they had.

Or so I thought.

The next morning, the husband guy was with her again. Same for the morning after that and every other weekday morning for two weeks.

Instead of being happy and fulfilled like I had been every weekday for half a freaking year, I got angry and resentful.

The next day, I got off at her work stop and followed her. I was planning to finally speak to her when she turned and came up to me and hugged me. I was stunned into silence.

"I'm so sorry. I know you must hate me and I can't blame you. My husband's hours at work changed, so he started riding the train with me. I don't want to, but how could I tell him not to? I'd be happy to travel with you on any day he stays home sick. Otherwise, I don't know how we can keep making this work." Before I could suggest it, she said, "I ride the subway home with a friend from work, so switching our time won't make any difference. Being with you made my commute so wonderful. Thank you."

That's when I got my first and only kiss from her on the lips. It's also when I whispered my first words to her. "I love you."

Unfortunately, she had already run off and didn't hear me.

My love was true, so I wasn't about to give up so easily. I kept going to her station every morning for two months, but her husband had some kind of super constitution because he didn't take a single day off in all that time.

I considered getting my hands on some form of germ warfare to make the guy stay home, but I have no connections in the microbiology community. I thought about picking dirty tissues out of a sick co-worker's garbage can but couldn't figure out how to expose Hubby to it. I've even contemplated knocking him off, but it sort of feels wrong. But I've gone from getting it five days a week to zero and I am not happy about it. Do you have any suggestions on how I can get my perfect woman back?

–Subway Woman Rider in Sunnyside

Dear Subway,

Ignoring the fact that one day all humanity shall be Cthulhu's property and that by killing the husband you would be stealing from me, getting away with murder is not as easy as many people think. Especially for those who don't have the temperament to hold up under police scrutiny or the intelligence to plan a killing without implicating themselves. You appear to have neither.

While your relationship with this woman is covert and the police may not be able to connect you to the crime, his wife might, which more than likely would end your commuter liaisons anyway, assuming she didn't point the police in your direction.

If I may suggest an alternative? Go to what is known in the vernacular as a strip club. There you can pay a woman to give you what is known as a lap dance. Given your sensitivity, this would likely be enough to take care of your needs and could also give you some variety, as you could engage the services of a different woman each night. Perhaps this will help you to avoid forging what would likely be a one-sided emotional connection like you did with Bootylicious, who is still a total stranger to you after months, yet still allow you to arrive at the same end result.

Dear Cthulhu,

I work for my local highway department. I've never gotten along with my supervisor, so he always makes me the flagger. Basically, I stand in front of oncoming traffic wearing a neon green vest and waving an orange flag.

Don't get me wrong. It's an extremely important job. You would not believe the number of idiots who ignore the slow signs. Working on an active highway repair site is a dangerous job and when these inconsiderate morons don't slow down, there's an increased risk of them hitting one of our crew and that can be fatal.

The problem is it's boring standing in one spot for eight hours waving a flag. I originally joined the highway department because I wanted to work with the big machines. My dream job is driving the steamroller but there are all these stupid regulations like having the right training plus things like seniority.

To help pass the time, I bought an old-fashioned boombox at a garage sale along with like a hundred cassette tapes. The whole thing set me back ten dollars, so I don't care when one of the driving simpletons accidentally hits it. It was made in the seventies and can stand up to any punishment a modern car can dish out. Unfortunately, it's also where my current predicament started.

I love music. If it has a beat, I have trouble standing still. I can't just tap my feet—I've got to dance. Now, I don't neglect my duties or anything like that. I simply dance with the flag and move it with the beat to get people to slow down. And you know what? It works. You know how people slow down and rubber neck to see an accident? The same logic applies here. People see me dancing and slow down to see what's going on. Which is great, because if they slow down, it's safer for me and the rest of my crew. Plus, folks seem to love it. They smile and wave as they pass. I've had to put out a tip bucket because people were throwing money out of their cars. I even went viral a few times on MeTube.

The dancing has made a boring job fun. Some of the other workers get down to the music with me.

The problem is my supervisor doesn't like it. He was some sort of tap dance prodigy back in the day, but it's hard to make a living tap dancing so he had to give it up and get a real job. It just burns him up that my amateur dancing is getting all this attention and the grump told me to stop.

My boss even tried to make something out of the fact that I'm getting tips and saying that it's not allowed, but I checked my employee handbook and there is nothing in it against accepting tips. It has never been an issue before because normally nobody wants to tip the people slowing down traffic and making them late for work.

It's not like it's a lot of money and I always use the cash to buy everybody (even my boss) coffee. If there's enough money, I spring for lunch on Fridays, so I'm not even keeping the cash for myself.

I've considered quitting and trying to use my Internet fame to get rich, but I was at least smart enough to try before I left my job. Know what I found out? People were more than willing to turn in to watch a two-minute video of some guy dancing on the side of the highway, but outside of some local news shows, nobody cared. No one wanted to pay money to buy a ticket to see me dance.

I need this job. It pays well and when I retire, I get a pension. What can I do to get my boss off my back?

–Dancing Dave in Dalton

Dear Dancing,

This is another thing Cthulhu does not understand about humans. You are all but insignificant dust in the cosmos and one asteroid or Cthulhu getting a cold and sneezing at a group of you would be enough to wipe you off the planet. Meanwhile, the lot of you are trying to destroy your planet in a dozen different ways from climate change and secret self-destructive messages hidden in K-pop music up to nuclear annihilation. Instead of being kind and understanding or trying to take care of each other, most humans simply are miserable to their fellow humans and work hard to make others' lives as sad as their own.

What difference does it make if you get a little attention dancing? In the overall view of the cosmos, less than nothing. However, your boss has the most dangerous and disheartening of all human conditions–he has a *dream*. Worse, a nonsensical dream of making it big as a tap dancer, despite the fact that no one has made it big by tap dancing as a career in decades. He has more chance of becoming a milkman or opening a photo booth.

Still, it is something he wants, and he has allowed himself to become deluded into thinking it could actually happen. Then he sees someone else, a subordinate no less, achieving something very close to his dream. Someone who didn't put in a fraction of the time or work that he did. It makes your boss feel as if he's even more insignificant than the rest of you humans and that he wasted much of the little life that he had available to him to chase an unobtainable dream. In situations like these, one must either have power over him or figure out a way to appease him. Since you have no power, consider instead working to make him feel appreciated for his dancing. Invite him to dance with you. Ask him to teach you how to dance better. Then arrange to have someone take a video on a day when the two of you are dancing together to slow traffic. Ask him to have a dance-offs which you then post on the internet.

Better still, give him credit. You bring up an excellent point about the danger people in your profession face when drivers do not slow down. Your dancing has worked in having people decrease their speed at your worksites. Make a video showing the success of the dancing, contrasting it to just waving a flag alone. Then say it was all thanks to your boss.

With luck, the new videos will get views and he will get credit. Better still, he will get to tap dance while being paid. You will have helped him achieve his unobtainable dream. Instead of vexing him, he will thank you, as long as you don't show him up. Take a dive for most of the dance-offs.

Or just accidentally trip him in front of ongoing traffic just enough that he gets put out of commission. Just be careful not to be caught, so do not do it while anyone is filming.

Dear Cthulhu,

I went to college at fourteen. I was no genius, but my parents were making me crazy by forcing me to be their servant. By ten years old, I was cleaning the house, doing the laundry, cooking the meals, washing the cars every day, and detailing them once a week. By twelve, I was feeding them (literally, like pretending the fork was a choo–choo and putting the food in their mouth). I had to brush and feed their pet llama, who they constantly told me was their favorite child. When Llama Larry pooped in the house, they blamed me, saying that I must have done something to upset the fleabag because Larry would never do something so crass. At fourteen, my parents decided they (and the llama) were going to start wearing adult cloth diapers and it would be my job to change then clean them and the diapers.

It was either run away and live on the streets or get into college. Being homeless was less than appealing, so I worked hard and got a full scholarship.

I had a blast. Maybe too much of a blast. Being tall for my age and having hit puberty early, I didn't look like fourteen, which helped me fit in with the older kids. My grades were good and I made the dean's list every semester. I even had a couple of girlfriends who had no idea how young I was. But my real undoing was alcohol.

I have to be honest—for the first couple years of college, I didn't touch the stuff. It wasn't for any moral reason. I just saw how stupid everybody else acted when they got drunk and I didn't want to be like that. I was probably self–conscious about my age, too.

That all changed one night at a frat party. I asked for an iced tea and accidentally got one of the Long Island variety. I chugged that sucker down, followed by another three, and that's all she wrote.

I woke up the next morning in a tree, wearing a doily as a thong and a clown mask, covered in plastic wrap, with thigh-high fishing boots with a hangover that made me question my life choices. I vowed then and there that I'd never drink again. That sacred vow lasted only until the next party.

Soon I got a fake ID and was drinking heavily. Oddly enough, my grades didn't suffer. All would've been fine except my college was doing one of those community–building activities during the Olympics where they were having the actual Olympic torch run through the town to pass prominent homes and businesses, carried by prominent folks. The entire student body was asked to gather along the campus portion of the run to cheer on the retiring dean of students. One of my friends dared me to strip down and streak alongside her, then take the torch from her and finish the run. At four Long Island iced teas in, it seemed like a great idea.

It wasn't hard. She *was* seventy, so I was able to catch her and snatch the torch with relative ease. I've got to give that lady credit, though—she chased after me for a while before giving up.

I was partway across the quad before the campus police joined in the chase. Sadly, they were a lot faster than the dean.

I tried to outrun them, but they had cars with lights. I realized cars couldn't go into buildings, so that's where I went.

It wasn't my proudest moment. I was too drunk to realize

that carrying a lit torch over my head while running through buildings was a bad idea. I set three of them on fire and burned down a kid's lemonade stand.

Needless to say, they caught me. I had climbed on top of an old-fashioned phone booth the town kept because they still do contests to see how many college students can fit in it. I wouldn't come down, so campus security grabbed my ankles and pulled me off. I fell, smashing my face and breaking my nose. Then, wearing a black plastic garbage bag and my face covered in blood, I got dragged to the college president's office. Turns out that video has almost as many hits as the ones of me streaking.

They wanted to expel me. Even drunk, I knew enough to demand a lawyer, so instead they had me arrested. The cops gave me a breath test and I blew 0.15.

I'm sitting in jail. My public defender is letting me borrow his laptop while he plays Kandy Smosh on his phone. I don't have enough money for bail and my parents won't help me. In fact, they and Llama Larry are disowning me, but that's the only good to come out of this.

Jail might be easier than the house I grew up in, but I still don't want to go.

What can I do to get out of this?

–Olympic Streaker

Dear Streaker,

Stop worrying about being arrested and expelled and start thinking lawsuit. Since much of this, including your injuries at the hands of the security guards, is caught on video and the police have your alcohol level documented, the university cannot dispute either. Your attorney can promise you will talk to the news, podcasts, and go on the talk show circuit, telling everyone who will listen about how this fine university neglected a child, which led you to become a teenage alcoholic for several years while living at their institution. That, in fact, their policies helped pour the alcohol down your throat to the point where you, a poor child, could no longer control your actions, which literally exposed you to the world. Then they left fire unprotected in a place a drunken child could reach it. What did they expect would happen? There was no reason to have their security guards smash that drunken child's face into a sidewalk from a height of seven feet (the height of an old–fashioned phone booth, in case you were wondering).

Such a story could keep a lot of parents from sending their children to a school that lets things like that happen to underage students. It could make enrollment numbers crash, which will hit them in the wallet. They should be willing to drop all charges in exchange for you keeping your mouth shut. You should be able to get a large cash settlement as well. If they argue about the fire damage to the buildings, have your lawyer point out they have insurance which will allow them to rebuild back, bigger and better. In short, you should come out a winner.

Dear Cthulhu,

I hate my life. I hate my wife. The first is mainly due to the second.

We've been happily married for two years. The problem is we wed fourteen years ago.

No matter what I do, my wife doesn't have a kind word for me, but has an unlimited supply of unkind ones. As far as she's concerned, I can't do anything right. Sometimes even my breathing bothers her.

She constantly bosses me around and micromanages every aspect of my life, from how I park my car to the way I hold the tissue when I blow my nose. I am so freaking depressed that I didn't know what to do until I saw an internet ad banner for a colonizing company.

Have you ever heard of these folks called the Man2Moon Foundation? They're working to build a colony on the moon and another one on Mars. They are supposedly very serious about it and have raised tens of millions of dollars. They are even offering colonists three thousand dollars upfront to sign on to go to the moon and ten grand to go to Mars. They just need one hundred people evenly divided between men and women for each. The catch on the Mars colony is that it would be a one-way trip. The people involved would never be able to come home again.

You can see why that appeals to me. I'd be so far away from my wife that she would never be able to bother me again. It would be like a little piece of heaven.

Of course, no situation is perfect. The contract is pretty ironclad and if I don't go, I'd have to pay back ten times what they give me, so a hundred thousand dollars instead of ten thousand.

If I'm being honest with myself, I'd have to admit that I work a low-paying job without any better prospects. I wouldn't be able to live in the house I do or have nice things if it wasn't for my wife's income. That's part of why I haven't left or divorced her. She was smart enough to make me sign a prenup. If we split, I get nothing. But if I went to Mars, the foundation would make sure I had everything I needed. Plus, living on another planet kind of sounds like fun.

But there is one reason I can think of where I wouldn't want to go and that's if it takes them so many years to get this expedition up and running that my wife passes away. If she's dead, I inherit everything. I'd have no reason to leave the planet. Unfortunately, the women of my wife's family are long-lived. Her grandmother made it to one hundred and seven. Her mother is in her 80s. They all have similar bossy personalities, so it isn't very surprising that the men in the family all died young. Natural causes are probably out, but there are always natural disasters and accidents.

Is it worth the risk to pay back that much money if my wife dies and I don't want to go?

–Rather Be On Mars Than In Mesa With My Mrs.

Dear Mars,

Cthulhu must admit this is the first I have ever heard of this. First off, make sure it is not a scam where in order for them to give you the money, you have to give them your credit card or bank number before you get the money. Two, while Earth does have the technology to get to both the moon and Mars, building a colony on either would not only be difficult, but incredibly expensive. It would cost tens of billions, if not trillions, to make it happen. Tens of millions are not going to get you much past the stratosphere. Perhaps this company is looking to lure more investments by showing them they have hard–core colonists who have foolishly sold their futures for a paltry sum in the hopes that such desperation might be taken for dedication and encourage the wealthy to part with significant investment capital. After all, one hundred people at ten thousand apiece is only one million for Mars and three hundred thousand for the moon. Not much of an investment for a serious startup.

And if the project somehow managed to literally get off the ground, it would give you a way out of your marital situation without actually breaking your vows, something Cthulhu is a stickler about.

However, you are thinking too small. There is a solution that would assure you that you get to stay on Earth and be separated from your wife, whether she lives or dies. Simply come up with a ruse to trick *her* into signing the colonist contract herself. From the way you describe your relationship, I highly doubt she lets you sign any legal documents by yourself. Since the money does not seem to be a priority for you, hire an unemployed actor or actress to play the part of an attorney. Have them call her and tell her that she received a $10,000 inheritance, but she needs to sign some paperwork to get it. You can go online to many legal sites and download realistic-looking forms that may or may not actually be legally binding. Have the actor give her a ridiculous number of papers to sign and hide the contract near the end but without placing it last. That way she will hopefully be tired of reading and simply sign. Have a video taken of her signing the contract. Have another of the documents allow the check to be given to and cashed by you. Buy a money order to give to her.

She would be happy because she thinks she's gotten a small windfall and if this company someday actually manages to achieve their goal, she shall be forced to go or give them the money. And if she's dead, they won't be able to enforce the contract. In fact, if you're smart, you'll tell her she inherited five grand, keep five for yourself, and pay the actor out of that. Consider inserting another contract rider to void your prenup and you can leave her now, but hire an actual lawyer for that so it will hold up in court when she challenges it.

Dear Cthulhu,

I'm a poor student. Not poor grade-wise. It's just that I don't have a lot of money because my parents won't give me any. They are always whining about all the money they're paying for my college tuition. And only my tuition, not my housing. Because of that, I have to live in a rundown rat trap that I can't afford. My friends made fun of me all semester because my only furniture was a couple of lawn chairs in the living room, a wobbly card table that I eat off, and a mattress that was left in the apartment when I moved in.

Last week when I was out walking—because surprise, surprise, my parents didn't buy me a car—I spotted a leather couch in pretty decent shape that'd been put out on the sidewalk next to some garbage cans. It seemed like a waste to leave it to be taken to the dump, so I called a buddy of mine. He came with his pickup truck and we loaded the couch in the back and brought it into my apartment. All was good for a couple of days and then I started noticing a smell. I lifted a couch cushion and found out two things, one cool and the other less so. The couch folded out into a bed and someone had stashed a dead body inside it. The corpse was wrapped in clear plastic bags, but one of the bags had a hole in it and the stench was leaking out.

Now I'm stressing because I've got a dead body in my apartment. And worse, I may end up losing my couch.

I don't know what to do. I mean, I don't want to live with a dead body, but giving up my only piece of actual furniture seems unthinkable. It's so much nicer than my two lawn chairs.

Should I figure out a way to take the body out and dump it? Or maybe take the couch to where I found it and put it back? I absolutely hate to basically yeet such a nice piece of furniture, but I don't want to go to jail. What should I do?

–College Student Cohabitating With A Couch Corpse in Colorado Springs

Dear Couch,

If your main concern is not getting arrested, then I suggest not moving either the body or the couch. By doing that and not alerting the authorities, you become complicit in the crime. While what they charge you with may not be murder, it could still be enough to land you in jail. The same goes if you move just the body or the couch with the body. However, they do provide you with a cot and toilet, so you wouldn't have to worry about furnishings.

The solution with the least risk in this case is to simply call the police and come clean. Explain what you did and then take them to where you found the body and they will investigate from there. They will ask a lot of questions and you will initially be a suspect, but if your friend with the pickup truck and your other friends who made fun of your furniture back you up, it will give your story more credibility. They will, however, take the couch and the body as evidence.

However, I have noticed a trend among humans lately to go on to a website like PayForMyCrap to set up a fundraising page where they convince people to pay for their rent, breast enhancements, dream vacations to New Jersey or, worse, some screenplay project they're working on.

A story like yours is bound to create at least a little media and internet coverage. Explain that all you wanted was a couch and what you got was a dead body. Plug your fundraiser, then perhaps total strangers will give you money as an amusement factor or out of some misguided altruistic intention to help others. Then you can buy another couch and maybe even some other furniture, although before you take it home, I recommend you check under the cushions.

Dear Cthulhu,

I read past letters from people who wrote you because they knew that they were supposed to be a Viking and a racecar driver. I am in a similar predicament. I know in my heart that I'm really a surgeon, but none of my friends or relations will let me operate on them. They make a big deal about me not having gone to med school, my lack of a license to practice medicine, and having no access to a sterile operating room like a hospital. I point out to them that for hundreds of years, doctors and even barbers operated on people without any of that stuff.

Even my own mother wouldn't let me operate on her when her appendix burst. I mean, it's a fairly simple operation and I've watched a guy do it on MeTube like three times. I could've done it easy, but no, Mom had to go to a real surgeon. I won't lie. That lack of faith in me has put a strain on our relationship, but I haven't cut off all ties because she's getting older and she'll likely need more surgeries as time goes by. Maybe she'll come to her senses and let me do them. Or maybe she'll make me her medical proxy and give me power of attorney and then I can give myself permission to surgerize her.

What I need from you is a way to fix it so people will let me operate on them. I was thinking I could move to a place where nobody knows me, rent a storefront, put up a sign, and just tell people I'm a doctor and operate on everyone. Heck, until I got good at it, I wouldn't even charge the people or bill their insurance. I'd consider it an even swap–the experience for me and the saving of money and co-pays for them. With the state of the healthcare industry, there'll be no better deal in the country.

So what do I need to do to make my innate surgerizing rights a reality?

–Natural Born Surgeon In St. Paul

Dear Natural,

Cthulhu again finds himself having to repeat what I have already stated. Humans have no innate rights that grant them the ability to be whatever they want. If they are fortunate on many fronts, they may have the opportunity to work toward something they would like to achieve, but even with the hardest of work, achieving a goal is never guaranteed.

The idea that just because you feel that you should be something doesn't mean that it should, could, or will happen.

Do you want to know the best way for people to allow you to operate on them? Go to college, get good grades, take the MCATs, and apply to med schools. If you get in, study, and work hard. Then, in several years, you will be a surgeon at which point people will let you operate on them—as opposed to "surgerizing" them.

Do not go ahead with your plan. Cthulhu's long-standing policy is that humans should not kill humans. That right is reserved only for Cthulhu. If you were to cut someone up in an incompetent and moronic attempt to perform surgery with no practical knowledge would, in all likelihood, result in the death of that person and the loss of my future property, slave, and/or meal. And more than likely you would end up incarcerated on charges, the least of which would be practicing medicine without a license.

If you want to simulate surgical acts, there are companies that make synthetic cadavers for medical students to work on. If you have the means, purchase one and use that to get these urges out of your system. If you are on a budget, buy the old board game where you use a pair of tweezers to pull organs out of a cartoon man. If you make a mistake, it will only buzz, not leave you with someone screaming in agony.

If all that hard work is not for you, consider joining the Cult of

Cthulhu. We have regular human sacrifices and—believe it or not—there are humans who are reluctant to cut up and slaughter others of their kind, even with the magnificent Cthulhu's permission. You will get to do something you want and Cthulhu will own you, body and soul. It is a win-win.

Dear Cthulhu,

I read with interest your response to *Subway Woman Rider in Sunnyside* and your suggestion that he have his needs met through lap dances at strip clubs. I've been doing this for years and have been very happy with the results. To max out my pleasure, I came up with this amazing hack—I wear sweatpants. It is brilliant and makes my time in the champagne room so much more enjoyable and intimate.

All was well until I focused all my attention on a dancer named Honeyshaker.

You'd think a worldly guy like me who goes to the club every night and tips well would be a little more popular with the dancers. Well, you'd be way wrong. Turns out the whole sweatpants hack skeeves them out. I'm not sure what they have to complain about. Lots of times they don't even have to give me the lap dance for the full time. I mean, they know when I'm done, if you get my drift. It really ruins the afterglow when they climb off my lap and grimace at me in disgust.

That's why I started going almost exclusively to Honey. She didn't seem to mind and always gives me a sexy look at the end as she dismounts. That extra bit of customer service made me feel close to her, like we had a bond. I even upped my tips to her by eleven percent.

The situation was ideal, at least until last night. During our nightly lap dance, Honeyshaker dropped a bombshell in my lap and not the good kind. Honey said she was pregnant and that the baby was mine. I told her she was full of crap because we'd never had sex. I mean, who needs that kind of hassle and cleanup when I get everything I need from the lap dances? It was about the same price as having a girlfriend without all the work, having to talk and feign interest. And my strip club expenses are a fraction of what divorce has cost a bunch of my buddies. Plus, I sell Pokey-A-Guy collectibles on U-Bay and ask the dancers for sales advice—most of it sucks but Honey had one helpful suggestion about using a fake account to drive up auction bids— so I can deduct the lap dances as expenses.

Honeyshaker countered my non-banging observation by saying that my love juice must have soaked through my sweatpants, which let my swimmers paddle their little tails hard enough to reach her fallopian tubes.

Honeyshaker claims she doesn't want anything to do with me other than paying her child support. First off, I'm not convinced that what she's saying could really happen. But after thinking about it for a while, I didn't hate the idea. It might be nice to have a little version of me around to play catch with and take out to the strip clubs when he is old enough, like ten or eleven or so, and get him his first lap dance. Not at his mom's club, obviously. Going to a strip joint and seeing his mom shaking her money maker would mess a kid up. Don't ask me how I know, but trust me on this.

I was thinking maybe I could woo Honey, then we could tie the knot. After all, I don't want any kid of mine being a bastard. Even if we were just married for an hour during the time he was born, that would eliminate the bastard thing and make the kid's life a little easier.

Do you think that's a good idea?

– Champagne Room Romeo Who May Have Popped His Cork One Time Too Many

Dear Cork,

Although it is unlikely, it is theoretically possible that you got Honeyshaker impregnated via a lap dance. What is far more likely is this woman became pregnant by another and sees you as a way for her to get paid for the next eighteen to twenty-one years by telling you this tale. To decide on the best course of action, you must determine the truth.

First, verify that she is truly pregnant. Testing sticks can be bought at any drug store. As it is unlikely that she will allow you to observe the process, it may be prudent to have a female of your species that you trust observe her discharge her urine directly upon the stick to reduce the risk of chicanery. If she is indeed with child, then insist upon a paternity test. With the advances in genetic testing, it should be fairly easy to determine whether her offspring is genetically yours. If it is, then you will have to determine what the best course of action to follow is, whether it be pursuing a more traditional romantic relationship with this woman or not. One thing to keep in mind is that if she actually agrees to a marriage, in your state, she will be entitled to half of your property. I would recommend getting a prenup prior to matrimony.

If the testing shows that are not the father, you would be wise to consider seeing another dancer to fulfill your need and start using some form of protection so that this unlikely event does not actually happen. If the traditional prophylactic is not to your liking, try placing a liquid–proof layer between your undergarment and sweatpants.

Dear Cthulhu,

I'm a 14-year-old boy who was born the wrong species. People see me as human when the reality is that in my heart and soul, I know that I am truly a dog, specifically a corgi.

I've seen stories on the internet about how girls who identify as cats have demanded their schools put litter boxes in the girls' bathroom for them.

That got me thinking. It's not fair that Feline–Americans get litter boxes in the schools, but there's nothing for us Canine–Americans. Don't get me wrong. I don't want a litter box.

I want a fire hydrant.

Now I'm a realist and know the school's not going to install special plumbing just for me, but in the long run, it doesn't have to be a working fire hydrant. I was thinking we could just put it in one of the shower stalls in the boys' locker room and I could pull the curtain when I use it to give me some privacy. I know I'm a dog trapped in a human body, but I have a shy bladder.

The principal said no the first time I asked, but I wasn't the only one he turned down. There's a girl at my school, "Felicity," who's Feline–American and they refused to put a litter box in for her too. She's pretty nice for a cat. We have a lot of fun with me chasing her around the school and up trees and then calling the fire department to get her down. The fire department seems less than thrilled though.

Felicity started a petition to get the support of other students to get her litter box but so far she's only gotten two signatures—hers and mine.

I didn't bother with a petition as I'd also only get two

signatures. Instead, I met with the principal again but this time I prepared. I explained what I wanted and pointed out to him that the Declaration of Independence states that every American is entitled to life, liberty, and the pursuit of happiness. I told him that this was my life, that my liberty would be infringed upon if I wasn't allowed to do it, and that having my own fire hydrant for my restroom breaks would definitely make me happy.

My principal countered by saying that only humans were guaranteed rights under the laws of the country and if I was identifying as a dog then those laws wouldn't apply.

I hate to admit it, but it was a damn good argument. I didn't have a good comeback without admitting I was really a person and therefore didn't need a fire hydrant.

My principal told me to have a good day and get back to class.

I was pissed that I couldn't piss where I wanted to. It wasn't fair but I'm a high school freshman. How the heck was I going to overrule the principal? I wasn't, but that didn't mean I had to roll over and play dead.

I struck back using the ancient ways of my people. Since my principal didn't keep slippers around and wore his shoes while he was in school, I couldn't chew them up. If I chowed down on his shoes while they were on his feet, he'd more than probably notice. So, I came up with a better plan.

The principal does a walk through the cafeteria during my lunch to say hi to the students every day at exactly 10:37 so I got the bathroom pass to leave the cafeteria before he got there and headed to his office. He had a door that opened onto the hall that he never locked because of his open-door policy so I snuck in that way. Like any dog trying to make a point, I peed on the corner of his desk. My urine ran down to get absorbed by his carpet. I snuck back out and returned to the cafeteria. I did this for a couple of weeks. The kids who got in trouble and were sent to his office said the place reeked of pee. I figured I'd taught him a lesson. If I was smart, I would have stopped there and gotten away with it.

Instead, I kept using his desk as my personal fire hydrant. But just because he was too ignorant to give me a fire hydrant didn't mean he was stupid. The principal knew someone was peeing in his office so he set up a surveillance camera to catch what the students were calling the Midnight Pisser. Admittedly, they got the time wrong, but it was still a cool name.

Unfortunately, that Monday when I went walkies to do my business, the principal captured it all on video. I got called into his office and enjoyed the stink until he called me a sicko and said that he should rub my nose in what I had done. That would have been okay with me because that would mean he accepted me for the dog that I really am.

My mom was majorly mad over everything and sent me to my room while she lavished affection on her dog Mr. Fuzzybottom, who also was a corgi. Don't read too much into that. It's not like I'm acting this way so I can get my mother's attention or anything like that. That would just be ridiculous, even more ridiculous than that she loves Mr. Fuzzybottom more than she loves me, her own flesh and blood. No, it's not something I think. Mom tells me that outright at least once a week and asks why I can't be more like Mr. Fuzzybottom. Mom said it again when she sent me to my room.

I didn't mind. I have my own doghouse in my room. Well, it used to be Mr. Fuzzybottom's but Mom decided it was too small for her fur baby so she got him a two-story doghouse with hot and cold running beef broth and a jacuzzi.

I'd asked to keep my hand–me–down doghouse in the yard but Mom didn't want the neighbors to see it and think we were weirdos. It's not like she doesn't dress Mr. Fuzzybottom in a different set of clothes every day for his walkies and then feeds him steak she cooks herself while I get hotdogs that I have to microwave myself.

Mom won't even get me a lawyer to help defend my civil rights. I contacted the ACLU they said I should probably call PETA, who hung up on me. I'm suspended pending an expulsion hearing. I suggested Mom homeschool me. She said no way. Then I suggested she send me to the same obedience school and puppy daycare that Mr. Fuzzybottom goes to. She said that it was too expensive to waste that kind of money on me. I called a bunch of lawyers around town and none of them would take my case without me giving them a lot more money than my allowance would cover.

Worse, now that I'm home, Mom's making me take care of Mr. Fuzzybottom.

I tried chewing up Mom's best six-inch stiletto heels and blaming it on Mr. Fuzzybottom but she blamed it on me instead saying Mr. Fuzzybottom would never do such a thing. And that the bite marks were that of a human, not a dog. I argued that identification by bite marks was considered junk science but it didn't make a difference. The next day I put steak sauce on another pair of her designer shoes and recorded Mr. Fuzzybottom chewing them to shreds. She refused to believe the video evidence and said I had created a deep fake. I showed her the shoes. Mom said that instead of filming Mr. Fuzzybottom, I should have taken the shoes away. Because it was my fault, she was docking my allowance for the rest of high school to pay for the shoes.

Mom's even making me take him for "walkies" and cook the dog's steak for him but I'm not allowed to have any of it. She checks my breath to see if I ate any. School breakfasts and lunches were the only decent food I got. It's why I'd rather go back to school even if I had to pretend to be human to graduate, but the principal's not budging.

What can I do to get back into school?

– The Midnight Pisser

Dear Pisser,

I am continually amazed by the fragility of the human psyche. It is obvious from your letter that your fixation on your species identity is a direct result of your mother's lack of affection and horrid child-rearing skills. You need to realize that transforming yourself into a pretend dog is not going to make your mother care about you any more than she does, which is sadly far less than the affection and caring she has for your family pet.

You are lashing out in a rather bizarre way in an attempt to get adult attention. Sadly for you, it has not worked out but kudos on the originality of your methods. I suggest you give up on finding an adult to love you, at least for now. Thanks to your mother, your ability to socialize with others appears to be stunted. Instead, focus on your friend Felicity. You appear to have delusions in common and perhaps you can become a support system for each other.

Also, if your mother is not there, eat some of the steak and soak some of your hot dogs in the steak dripping and see if the dog will eat it and therefore not appear hungry. Then rinse your mouth out or drink something to cover the taste.

You have overlooked something very obvious in terms of forcing your way back into your school. At 14 years of age, you are a minor. Your principal set up a surveillance camera with the knowledge that someone was relieving their bladder in his office and that most of the suspects were high school students, the majority of whom are less than 18 years old. This means he recorded as you exposed a part of yourself that is illegal to be recorded. Simply tell your principal that you are making a Klik Klok video explaining how he purposely filmed a minor in a partial state of undress and then kicked you out of school for it. With the current prevalence of cancel culture in your society it is more than likely that such a video will go viral which could result in him being suspended or fired from his job.

If the man is intelligent and fearful enough, he will likely delete the video. Without the video, he has no evidence against you. Give him twenty-four hours to reinstate you to your high school. If he does not, record a video, including pictures of the front of your high school and your principal which are likely to be found on the school website or his social media. Send him the video before you post it. Let him know that a friend will be posting the video in twelve hours if they don't hear from you to stop it. This should show him that you mean business and discourage him from attempting to end your life in a bid to protect his job.

If he still refuses, post it. You will have more attention than you know what to do with.

Secretly record your mother telling you that you should be more like the family dog and you will likely go viral again and perhaps get more sympathy. Either way, you get more of the attention you crave. Also, it will come in handy later in life, especially during your inevitable therapy sessions.

In any interviews you end up doing, tell them that your mother trained you to become a Canine-American. She will either enjoy the notoriety and treat you better or be upset and give you more negative attention.

You may be able to trick your mother into getting you your fire hydrant at home. After taking Mr. Fuzzybottom for his "walkies," return telling your mother how much he enjoys stopping at all the fire hydrants and suggest that Mr. Fuzzybottom might like a plastic fire hydrant of his own in the backyard. As she actually likes the canine as opposed to her offspring, she will likely purchase one online. You can place it where you will not be seen and use it in private if you still feel the desire to empty your bladder that way.

However, if you are allowed back in school, use a urinal or toilet there from then on to avoid more problems and to keep the availability of your school meals. You could go to a printing website, have huge fire hydrant stickers made, and stick them on the inside of the school's urinals.

Also, you demonstrate the reason humans should not believe everything they see on the internet. You and Felicity are misinformed. Students who identify as cats being given their own litter boxes to use at school is an urban myth. There is no instance of this happening anywhere in your country but the fake story is spread by one ideological group attempting to make another look foolish and gullible humans, which is sadly a significant percentage of you, believe and spread it until people accept it as truth.

Dear Cthulhu,

I wrote you last year about how when my cheating boyfriend left me, I started a romantic relationship with a duck and rather enjoyed his corkscrew private bit until it came off during one of our lovemaking sessions. I appreciate you letting me know that a duck's penis can fall off every year and then grow back. I followed your advice regarding the fact that ducks' penises will grow back larger if they are around other male ducks.

I didn't feel comfortable bringing him to some pond in the woods where he might migrate away with some strange female duck. I also didn't want to bring him to the pond in the town park because when I left, people might think I was stealing him and report me to the police. Instead, I ran constant HD footage of male ducks while I was at work on my big screen TV using my surround sound system to carry their quacks and such. Because of the size of the TV, the ducks appeared to be several times normal size and I think I may have overdone matters because Mallard's member grew back with gigantic portions, easily beyond the size of a well-endowed man but it was still corkscrew-shaped.

The sex this year was so much better than last year, which even before was far better than it was with my ex. Also, probably because of the increased size, his penis stayed on for months this time. Mallard made me feel like more of a woman than any man ever had.

Sadly, just like last year, his beautiful member eventually fell off. I consoled myself ahead of time that at least this time I was prepared for it.

It turns out that I wasn't.

This time it detached during the largest climax I've ever had and something about my convulsions snapped it off.

This is where the bad part came in. My lady parts clamped down so intensely that I'm unable to remove Mallard's magnificent member.

I'm walking with my feet so far apart that I'm waddling. Is this why female ducks walk the way they do?

I'm too embarrassed to get medical help. How can I get Mallard's member out of me?

– Love A Duck and Stuck in Duluth

Dear Duluth,

Some might tell you to try to use cutting tools in order to snip the duck's procreational organ into smaller bits that could be more easily removed. Or they might suggest you soak yourself in something warm to soften the keratin that makes up the duck penis as well as relax the muscles in your body that are holding it in place. However, not knowing how proficient you are with tools and what your manual dexterity level is, I would recommend against any of that and strongly suggest that you go to your nearest emergency room to reduce your risk of permanent injury. I would normally comfort somebody in your situation by telling them that no matter how unusual their injury is, it is likely the emergency room staff have seen things far more bizarre. Sadly, in your case, I cannot but this is still the safest course of action for you to follow.

Next year if you choose to repeat the process, might I suggest using a smaller screen television so the ducks do not appear so much bigger than Mallard and the new penis does not grow so large.

An even more daring suggestion–why not consider returning to performing procreation activities with someone of your own species? If you have become fixated and fetishized on having a duck as a procreation partner, have the human male wear a duck suit or even just a duck mask that looks similar to Mallard. Such things can be found easily on the Internet. If there is one thing Cthulhu has learned about most human males is that they are willing to agree to just about anything that does not harm them, as well as several things that might, if the opportunity for procreating is made part of the deal. A good place and time to find one just for procreation is at almost any bar or club near closing time. You will likely have your pick of the men present.

Dear Cthulhu,

I think I'm in deep trouble. I got bit by a dog and I think it's going to turn me gay.

Let me explain. My buddy got a blue tick hound for breeding so his girl blue tick would get all knocked up and have puppies that he could sell. The only problem with his moneymaking scheme is that his dog "Humper" has no interest in his girl blue tick hound, only his other neutered boy dogs. He paid a ton of money and he's suing the breeder for selling him a gay dog.

He went away with his girlfriend for the weekend and asked me to look after his dogs. His house is nicer than my trailer and he's got a big-screen TV, so I said sure, even though I had to leave my cat, Flufflestiltskin, at home.

While I was making some dinner and smashing some ground beef into burgers, Humper started humping my leg. I reached down to push him off. Now, normally Humper's a nice dog. I don't know if it was because I had the meat juice on my hands but when my hand got close, Humber bit it and broke the skin.

The bite was bleeding pretty bad, so I wrapped a dishtowel around it but once I let go, the bite started bleeding again. I called a buddy of mine to take me to the emergency room.

On the way to the hospital "Talbot" tells me he had been watching a werewolf movie and that if I'd been bit by one I'd become a werewolf but because I was bit by Humper, I'd probably end up turning gay the next during the next full moon.

People at my church ain't real nice to the gays so I don't need those holy rollers lecturing me. Not that I have a problem with any folks mind you. What folks do in the privacy of their own bedrooms ain't none of my business and what I do in mine shouldn't be any of theirs. I only go to worship service on Sundays cause otherwise my ma and gram would be sad.

After the doc stitched me up, I asked if maybe I needed a shot or a vaccine. She asked why I'd need a vaccine because I had Humper's vet records and he'd had all his shots so I'd be okay with just antibiotics. I told her that I needed it so I didn't turn gay when the next full moon came out.

Let me tell you the doctor looked at me like my elevator didn't go all the way to the top floor. The doctor said that I didn't have to worry because neither a dog bite nor a vaccine can change somebody's sexual orientation.

I know all the doctors are in cahoots with the government and get like a grand anytime they inject somebody with one of those vaccine computer chips, so I don't know if I can trust what she said. But since she didn't shoot me up for the cash, so maybe she's a good one and ain't lying?

I don't want to mention this to anybody else I know, cause they might think I'm stupid or crazy but I figured ole Cthulhu would have the skinny. Is the doc lying to me? If she is, where could I get the vaccine? Will the microchip let me stream movies and stuff for free? Do I need a password for that? If I talk to the people listening in, will they talk back?

And if there ain't a shot, will I only turn gay when the moon is full? Cause that would be okay with me. I mean, I doubt it would improve my love life. I ain't all that attractive to women so I doubt men will suddenly think I'm a catch and fall for me just cause I switched teams, ya know?

There is one thing about turning gay that would be awesome. If I turn gay, do I get the gay powers? That'd be so cool. My trailer décor is a bit tacky and my fashion sense can't seem to reach past flannel and blue jeans. If I got the gay powers, I could give myself a makeover and maybe feel a little better about myself and make more than the three friends I've had since high school. If I dressed better and had a nicer haircut, I think I'd fit in better and people would like me more. Plus, it'd be nice to live in a place that looks nice. I think it would be better for my self–confidence and lower my anxiety level.

-Looking Forward To The Full Moon In Lansing

Dear Full,

When Cthulhu started reading your letter, I thought I would be dealing with a human of sub-average intelligence. Perhaps I am but you appear to be more likely of the type whose mind and thinking are easily manipulated by others. Please consider changing your house of worship to the Cult of Cthulhu. We can always use more people like you even if you do seem to have an optimistic bent, but that is something we can work on.

Your doctor was telling the truth. Human sexuality is not able to be altered by either a bite or a vaccine.

Also being gay does not automatically bestow improved taste and fashion sense in people. However, you can develop your own meager abilities in these areas. There are shows, videos, books, and magazines devoted to fashion that can help you learn. I suspect there are online and in-person classes as well. You can go to a store you consider fashionable and ask for their help in changing your style. Check out to see if there are any so-called influencers specializing in fashion who would do a makeover for you in exchange for being in their video, although be warned of scams. If you must pay for your new clothing, buy it directly from the store or website after checking to make sure the prices aren't exorbitantly elevated.

Put yourself in more social situations, particularly ones involving activities that you enjoy and perhaps you will end up interacting with more humans, although why you would want that is a mystery.

And if the above does not relieve your worries, allow yourself to be bitten by a male dog that has sired puppies. His bite should counteract any effect from the previous one.

Dear Cthulhu,

I am a devout Catholic. How devout? I consider the Pope a slacker. When I was a kid in Catholic school and they read us all the stories of the saints, I knew then and there that it was my destiny to join their number. Ever since, I've followed every rule of the church to the letter to make sure I qualified. Sure, there's the minor issue of me not having performed any miracles, but I'm hoping somehow that might be overlooked due to my amazing devoutness.

One of the most important religious seasons is, of course, Lent. It's a wonderful opportunity to show off just how devout I am in so many ways. It starts with me getting to wear ashes on my forehead. I don't wipe or wash them off and have managed to have my ashy mark last for three full days by sleeping in a recliner and strapping my head in place so I don't accidentally rub my forehead against anything that will knock the burned palms off.

Plus, on Ash Wednesday and every Friday for forty days (and nights) I get to abstain from eating meat. It's great fun being able to point this out to everyone at work plus letting everyone know that I fast between my two meals so I can't even have non-meaty snacks and I only have to fast on Ash Wednesday and Good Friday, so how's that for going above and beyond?

Just in case someone didn't know about my piety, I heat up the stinkiest fish available in the work microwave for lunch. The best part is that no one can complain because I would call them out on their religious discrimination. It's so great getting to rub their faces in how very devout I am.

My problem is my dog is making me look bad. "Heathen"

eats meat because that's what's in dog food. At least that's what it says on the label.

The brand I buy doesn't have true fish-only dog food because they add beef or chicken fat. Last time I checked, cows and chickens aren't fish so those are a no-go. I checked a few other brands and they all seem to do the same. Because abstinence from meat is also part of Fridays during Lent, I just stopped feeding him. It's obvious Heathen is not as devout as I am. The mutt spends the whole of Fridays whimpering and looking up at me with his big eyes as if that's going to change my mind about letting him eat the devil's kibble. I used to be married, but then I caught my wife eating a hamburger on a Friday during Lent and I divorced her quicker than you can say third circle of hell. That's where the gluttons go, by the way.

My ex argued that it was St. Patrick's Day and that the bishop had given dispensation for people to forgo the meatless aspect because of the holy day. What she said was true, but come on. That guy was only a bishop, not the Pope. Who gave him the right to say we can break holy law? Not me, that's for sure. And as a future saint, I think I'm a little better positioned than some loser who devoted his whole cushy life to the church instead of living a real life.

Now, I can hear you arguing that Catholics aren't allowed to get divorced and you're right. I got divorced civilly but paid extra to get an annulment from the Church. That means as far as religion is concerned, I was never married. Being single will probably help the whole getting canonized process anyway.

So if I'm going to get rid of my own wife for breaking holy

law, why would my dog think he was going to fare any better?

I'm trying to decide if I should give Heathen one more chance to get with the program or if I should drive him out to the country, then throw him out of the car so he can live on some atheist farm.

What do you think I should do?

–Future Saint In St. Louis

Dear Future,

The religion that you profess to be a part of is in direct competition with my own Cult of Cthulhu, the 12th fastest-growing religion in the world. Thus, Cthulhu can hardly be considered an expert on yours. Still, it seems that you are entirely missing the point of your church, one whose teachings are less concerned with shows of religious piety than with people helping the least fortunate of their fellows. Their words, not mine.

If you're going to go with a second-rate religion that thinks they are better than Cthulhu just because they have over a billion followers, the least you could do is perform its precepts correctly. You don't mention how you help out the sick, the poor, or anyone else for that matter. Do you even do charity work? I would guess not.

As for your dog, you are terribly misguided. There are very few creatures on this poor pitiful planet that give love unconditionally. That you would consider dumping such an animal as if it was yesterday's garbage is reprehensible and the very definition of unchristian.

Also, are you aware that strange dogs running up to a farm (atheist or otherwise) often end up chasing the farm animals and thus sometimes are shot by the farmer? Farms don't simply take in any animal that wanders by. Such matters need to be discussed and agreed to by the farmer.

I recommend you do the right thing and find a better home for your dog. Would your ex-wife consider taking Heathen? If not, check with people you know to see if they would adopt a dog. If worse comes to worst, take him to a no-kill shelter.

Also, your entire premise is faulty. Your church does not mandate meatless Fridays for everyone, It mandates abstinence from meat only for those older than fourteen. Those with health issues are exempted. Their rules say nothing about animals having to follow this tradition. In fact, since the rules mention years–not dog years mind you–I can only assume your dog is under the minimum age of fourteen and so would be exempt even if he was human. By way of contrast, the Cult of Cthulhu enforces no dietary restrictions. At least for me. I forget if I gave any to my worshippers.

And you are incorrect about yet another fact. The most important religious season of the year by far is Cthulhumas.

Finally, if you plan to continue to be self-centered and selfish, which I can only assume you will, consider feeding your dog canned tuna or some other seafood after checking with a vet that it will do the animal no harm.

Many people in your religion are pious. Being cruel to your pet does nothing to set you apart from them, so how can you truly expect to achieve sainthood? In your religion's history, they grant special recognition to martyrs, a great number of whom were granted sainthood. Have you considered martyrdom as an option? You need to go to some part of the world and convince or force others to join your religion. If you do it right, those people will be annoyed enough to kill you. Judging by your letter, I think you have an excellent shot at convincing other humans that they end your existence. I suggest trying out a war-zone and preaching to large groups with guns and other weapons. If you do, you will achieve martyrdom in no time,. You could even document your actions on social media to leave behind a firsthand account of your struggles and sacrifices for the saint maker board to consider.

If you lack the conviction or faith to go that route, consider trying to fake the mandatory miracle. Stigmata are big. Give the marks to yourself but claim no knowledge of where they came from. Work to keep them open and seeping. Sure, there is the risk of infection and death, but what is a little death if it helps you achieve your big goal of sainthood?

Mind you, you will be surprised by the reaction you get in the afterlife to your so-called devout life. At least Heathen can wag his tail at you from behind the Pearly Gates as all dogs go to Heaven. Fortunately for those like Heathen, not all their owners do.

Dear Cthulhu,

I read the letter from the *Midnight Pisser* and am writing to tell you that you're full of clumps! I've seen plenty of Klik Kloks, MeTube videos, and blog posts talking about all these kids like me who identify as cats and have made their schools install litter boxes for them to use during the day.

Honestly, if I was willing to drop my drawers in front of a bunch of judgmental teenage girls with cell phones, I'd make my school board put in one.

Unfortunately for me, somebody else decided to put in a giant litter box in my high school and it's made my life worse than coughing up a hundred and one fur balls.

I make no secret that I'm a Feline–American. I wear ears and a tail to school to identify with my people. Someone has to stand up and lead the way in making being a Feline–American normal and I have the courage to be on the front lines.

This means that my classmates and the rest of the school are all aware of how I identify. Sure, I get made fun of a lot, but I wear my nails long and instead of acrylic, my tips are stainless steel so no one takes it past mocking and teasing. At least not to my face. I like to refer to it as my own form of claw enforcement.

One of the reasons I know I'm a Feline–American is because I came across a big bag of leaves in my dad's sock drawer and I asked him what it was. His face turned pale and he grabbed the bag out of my hands and said it was catnip. Then he begged me not to tell my mom because he promised her he'd given it up. I asked him why she would care if he had catnip. Dad said it was complicated, but he'd give me a hundred bucks if I promised not to tell. I took the cash.

I figured my dad was in the cat carrier about being a Feline–American himself but I kept my mouth shut. I did start dipping into his catnip. It made me so relaxed and happy that all the stress from school disappeared. For a little while anyway. And since catnip only works on cats, that's when I realized that I was truly a Feline–American. I used the hundred bucks to buy my first set of cat ears and tail.

I loved the catnip so much that I started bringing a little with me to school. I eat a little bit of it throughout the day. Then somebody broke into my locker and stole it, which did not make me happy. I couldn't figure out who would do that since as far as I know I'm the only Feline–American in my school and what would a human want with catnip?

I reported to the office that somebody had stolen something out of my locker to see if they caught the thief on camera but it turns out the camera in that hallway is broken. To stop it from happening again, I bought and installed little spy cameras, one that could see through the vents in my locker to film the hall and hid it behind a picture of the winner of last year's East Minster Cat Show so no one could see it when the locker was open. The other I put in the back of the locker to record anyone stealing. Both are motion–activated.

The next morning before I could get close enough to use Bluetooth to upload the footage from the night before, I got called into the office. They accused me of installing a giant litter box in the first–floor girls' bathroom and then pooping and peeing in it.

I defended myself, saying I'd done no such thing. The Dean

of Students told me they had footage showing I was guilty. I told them that was impossible and that any footage would prove my innocence. They called up security video on the Dean's computer screen.

I said it was very creepy that they had cameras installed in the girls' room. They said they didn't, but they had footage of the person who'd brought in the litter and box into the school and the bathroom.

On the computer monitor, somebody in a giant cat suit walked in carrying what looked like a plastic kiddie pool and dragging a hundred-pound bag of kitty litter on a skateboard. The footage showed the person in the suit sneaking through the dark and empty halls to the girls' room. They came out sometime later without the kiddie pool or the kitty litter.

I said that it could be anybody in that suit. They said I was the only person at school who outwardly identified as a cat. I corrected their mistake and told them to call me a Feline–American but they didn't care. I also explained that I wasn't a furry–people who dress up in costumes and pretend to be animals as opposed to those who incorporate the essence of the animal into their daily lives without a suit. They pointed out that I wore cat ears and a tail. I said it wasn't the same thing, but they didn't see a difference.

I said there's no way they can prove it was me, which is when they said they found the cat suit in my locker. I told them I'd been framed and had already reported that someone had broken into my locker and stole from me so that same person could have broken into my locker and planted the suit.

The Dean said that seemed highly unlikely. I pointed out that if the cat suit was left in my locker, they must have footage of whoever was in the suit leaving the building. They said whoever did it must have walked out the exit on my locker hallway because they knew there was no camera there. Because of the theft, I knew the video surveillance was down and they claimed I took advantage of it.

It was totally ridiculous, so I demanded a hearing by the rules of the student handbook–I read everything–so they had to give me one. I have ten days to prepare my defense but I don't need one.

I went to my locker and downloaded the footage on my locker spy cameras. As soon as I fast-forwarded through it, I knew who framed me. It was Brandy, one of the girls who always makes fun of me. If her stepping out of the costume, putting it in my locker, then leaving was all that it showed, I would have immediately turned in the footage. It was more complicated and interesting than just that.

Let me preface this by saying that I am a cisgender Feline–American teenage female who is extremely hormonal, horny, and more than open to the idea of a trans-species tryst. Especially with Brandon, who despite publicly identifying as a human cisgendered male has a very obvious feline spirit and aura. I would give up catnip for a month for him to alley cat around with me for a night. Sadly, he's dating and banging Brandy, including right before she put the catsuit in my locker. That's right, Bradon came into the camera–free hall and smashed Brandy while she was still wearing the suit, even the head. They held their own private mating season right there against the water fountain. The suit had a section that snapped open for just such an occasion.

This footage will let me prove my innocence and lick Brandon up like a bowl of cream before riding him to downtown Pound Town without stopping until my thirst is satisfied.

My first thought was to steal the catsuit from the Dean's office, then show Brandy the footage. I'd promise not to turn the footage over to the Dean in exchange for two things. Brandy swearing that I was with her the entirety of the night in question and that she would arrange for Brandon to meet up with her in the catsuit again, only this time I'd be the one inside getting smashed.

My other thought was to turn in the footage of her getting out of the costume and putting it in my locker, then stealing my catnip, leaving out any bits showing Brandon. After Brandy gets expelled, I tell Brandon that I have the footage of his involvement, but I'll make sure the Dean never sees it in exchange for a little cat on a hot tin roof action. The problem with that is, I don't really think Brandon likes me. I'm afraid he might not be very excited about his cat call if you get my drift. But if he thinks I'm Brandy in the suit, he'd give me the same treatment and smashing he gave her which would be (dare I say it?) purrfect.

What's my best go to here?

–Framed Feline–American In Heat In Highlands Ranch

Dear Framed,

In this situation, your possession of the footage gives you a bit of power. It should go without saying (but having written this column for going on two human decades, I know that if things truly went without saying that Cthulhu would receive far fewer letters) but make sure you backup your footage to an external disk drive as well as the cloud.

You can do whatever you feel you can get away with, in exchange for whatever you think you can get. Be aware that there are several flaws with parts of your plans. You fail to mention the age of your classmates but if they are minors, having that footage could be considered a crime which could come back to scratch you in the tail.

Also in your culture, procreation without consent is not only looked down upon but can be considered a crime that can be prosecuted depending on the inclination of the local district attorney and, often, their reelection platform. Should you procreate with this Brandon while having him think you are someone else, while fun and exciting, could backfire and flip the power dynamic. Because that plan involves having Brandy arrange the meeting, it will allow her to take a page from your book and film the mating interaction. Then she would have blackmail material against you. The penalty a sexual crime carries is far worse than that of someone defecating in a plastic pool while in a cat costume.

Simply turning the footage of Brandy placing the costume in your locker may be the way to go with the least jail time for you. Cthulhu recommends you edit out any evidence of her stealing your "catnip" as the leafy substance is not what you believe it to be. It is something that was made legal in your state several years back, but only for those over the age of twenty-one. An age which you are not unless you have been held back for a number of years. Your father lied to you rather than telling you that you found his stash of marijuana. Now you can understand why he was willing to pay for you to not tell your mother.

You can still approach this Brandon without opening yourself up to being charged with a crime. After turning Brandy in, meet with Brandon privately and let him know you have the footage of him abetting Brandy's actions and that you are debating about turning that in too but wanted to give him a chance to offer you a reason not to. Mention that your cousin in another state has a copy of it and is waiting to post it. Allowing him to think that someone else besides you has the footage will make him less likely to kill you to stop you from turning it in. He may offer you his procreational services in exchange for not being expelled. Or he may offer you something else such as money. He may offer you nothing at which time you will have to decide what to do with that footage.

Dear Cthulhu,

I've never been very motivated in life, always traveling along the path of least resistance. This is probably why I've never held a job for longer than I needed to qualify for unemployment before I got fired.

My salary has never been impressive and unemployment benefits are even less so which forced me to supplement my income. I'm too lazy to go out and find a job that will pay me under the table, so instead I stand at a busy highway exit holding a cardboard sign asking people to give what they can while they wait for the red light to turn green. I usually make about a hundred a day, which isn't a lot but I don't pay taxes on it.

Standing all day is rough, I bring a folding sling chair to rest in. One day these two girls were walking home from school killing time and asked if they could sit by me. It seems they were locked out of their house until their mom got home from work and some other kids in the neighborhood were giving them a hard time.

I'm lazy, not heartless so I said sure. One sat on the ground and the other one in my chair. I asked them if they were hungry and shared snacks and drinks I kept in a cooler bag.

People noticed the kids and must have assumed they were mine. Folks who stopped to give me money were suddenly handing me tens and twenties instead of ones, fives, and spare change. I made four hundred bucks that day instead of a hundred.

I gave each of the girls a twenty and said if they wanted to come back tomorrow, I'd give them more money. I brought three chairs, a folding table, better snacks, and healthier drinks. The girls came after school and used the table to do their homework. I insisted upon that. Begging is okay for an after–school job but these kids were bright and were destined for bigger things than me. I even made a bigger sign that read *Please give money for food, clothes, and school supplies.*

I made five hundred that day and gave each of the girls forty bucks. This went on for more than a week until one day their mother showed up after she got out of work. Turns out the girls had told her what we were doing. I expected to get chewed out for taking advantage of her kids.

Instead, she took advantage of me. Mama sat down in my chair between the girls and made me stand. Since she was there, the girls were able to stay an hour and a half later. The take was over six hundred bucks.

The only problem was their Mama wasn't easily bought off with a couple of twenties. Mama said the three of them deserved fifty percent of the take.

I said no and that I should charge her for babysitting until she got out of work. She countered by saying that they were going to take a couple of days off and give me a chance to think about it. Without the kids, my earnings dropped back down to around 100 bucks.

Before the mother butted in, I was taking home over four hundred dollars a day. If I give into the mother's fifty-fifty split extortion, I'll only take home three hundred. I'll be losing a hundred bucks a day! That's five hundred a week.

I was thinking maybe I could get some picture cardboard cutouts of the kids and keep them up there. That way I wouldn't have to pay them except for the pictures. Or better yet, have them pose with me for a "family" portrait, blow that up to poster size, and put it on my sign.

I just don't think I should have to give up that much cash. Do you think people driving by would be fooled by the cutouts? Or would it be better to invest in a lifelike baby doll and carriage to prey on people's sympathies instead?

– Beggar Being a Chooser In The Bronx

Dear Beggar,

It appears you are not only lazy when it comes to work but also when it comes to math.

People will not be tricked by cardboard cutouts. They may even be turned off and not give you anything for trying to fool them. Same with using a toy baby doll which may even end with you being brought up on fraud charges.

The "family" picture on the sign might help but from a distance, people aren't going to be able to make out the details like they would with actual children sitting there.

Back to your math deficits. On your own, you are only making one hundred dollars a day. Forget what you were making before the mother got involved. That split is gone and not coming back. With the new deal comes extended hours for the girls' which appears to add to your income. If your numbers are correct and continue, at fifty percent, you will be taking home over three hundred dollars a day, an increase over your solo efforts of two hundred extra dollars a day.

Look at it this way—for doing the same amount of so-called work, figuring one hundred dollars a day as your solo base pay, you make five hundred a week. With your counterfeit family's assistance, that amount triples to three hundred a day and fifteen hundred dollars a week. You are effectively tripling your income. That is far better than what you can do on your own. The sympathy caused by the presence of the children (perhaps also the legitimacy of having their mother there as well) is crucial to your enterprise. The girls are this woman's spawn and she is within her rights to look out for their best interests.

If you do not take the deal that this woman is offering you,

you will you lose $1000 a week or–assuming you work without taking a vacation–$52,000 a year bringing your total annual take to $78,000 (instead of $26,00 without them). You may be lazy but that's no reason to be stupid as well. Take the deal.

Consider that you may be missing out on even more income. Make sure the children, their mother, and you wear raggedy clothing which you can make filthy-looking to garner even more sympathy from your marks. The clothing can be gotten inexpensively from your local Salvation Navy store. When all of you arrive to work, mess up everyone's hair. Use props like a bag of cans and bottles to have it appear as if you're collecting them for the deposit. Have the children draw cute pictures and tape them on the folding table with a sign saying "Art for $10". People may consider buying them. Play with the price to see what it sells best at. The children should be able to knock out plenty and with the low cost of paper and crayons, it should be easy to make a profit, which under your current deal you would get half of. Find ways to get fruit or bottled water at a discount and have the children sell it as you are too lazy to do it. You can even pick up some old toys at the Salvation Navy and put them out for sale. People will assume that things are so bad for your "family" that the children have to sell their toys. This will likely bring even more income as some people may insist that the children keep the toys and you can sell them multiple times. Here is where you can use a baby doll or stuffed animal to tug harder on people's heartstrings and convince them to open their purse strings. You need to realize that being smarter and planning will allow you to be lazy and make more money with a minor increase in effort.

Dear Cthulhu,

I live in a very conservative small town. Folks are real judgmental here of anything out of the ordinary. I'm not quite as judgmental as most of the folks around me but I don't exactly speak up against them either.

We had this one openly gay kid in my graduating class back in high school. He did not have an easy time in high school. They made his life a living hell. And by they, I mainly mean me. I tormented "Bruce" every chance I had and created a few chances when I didn't. Bruce left town the day after graduation and never came back. Not that I blame the guy.

Right after graduation, I started work driving a dump truck and I've done okay for myself. The only problem is that my mom and grandma had been riding me about finding myself a girlfriend and getting married providing them with some grandkids and great-grandkids.

The problem is I don't want any part of that. I realized when I was in middle school that I had no romantic interest in girls. Boys on the other hand… well, let's just say I had to work very hard not to stare in the locker room, especially when I played football. I was deathly afraid that someone would figure out that I was gay and make my life miserable. I guess that's why I was a total butt wipe and tormented Bruce so much. My teenage mind figured that if I kept everyone focused on him, they'd ignore me. Despite my tormenting, I didn't hate the guy. I admired him for having the courage to come out like that where we grew up. I wasn't brave like him in high school. Heck, I'm out of high school six years and I still don't have that kind of courage.

My story takes a little bit of a twist. Last month, I took a trip into the city and accidentally bumped into Bruce. He was scrawny back in high school but he had filled in and worked out. He was built like a movie star now.

It was obvious Bruce wasn't happy to see me and I couldn't exactly blame him. Maybe I didn't have his courage. but I had grown some since high school. I apologized for how I treated him and asked for his forgiveness. Bruce asked why I had been so cruel to him. I told him it was a long story. He said he was willing to listen, so we went to a coffee shop. I bought Bruce a cappuccino and told him the truth.

It was a huge relief to finally come clean about who I was. Bruce was so understanding. He told me he forgave me, and even gave me a hug. That hug led to a kiss and I ended up in his apartment losing my virginity. It was amazing. Well, at least at first.

It turns out Bruce coming on to me wasn't from any sense of passion or affection. In the afterglow, he told me how I'd made his teenage years a living hell and that he was still in counseling dealing with the psychological damage I caused. Bruce told me that I was a horrible person and he was only taking advantage of me. Then he topped it off by telling me I was terrible in the sack.

I went from deliriously happy to devastated but Bruce wasn't done. Oh no. He saved the worst for last–although telling me I was a horrible lover was a very close second.

Bruce let me know that he was going to tell everybody in our town that I was gay. I begged him not to. I told him I wasn't ready to have my family, friends, and church know. Bruce laughed and said, "It sucks to be you then."

I told him people would believe me over him and just think he was trying to get even for all my bullying. Bruce said that would probably be true if he hadn't recorded our tryst on his home security cameras and then showed me some of the footage on his cell phone. I was horrified by the betrayal of my privacy but as I watched, it looked to me as if I was doing a damn good job, particularly for my first time. And that was backed up by the expressions on Bruce's face. He said he faked it.

Turns out, Bruce wasn't bluffing. By the time I got home, he'd posted footage of us having sex on social media with enough of the naughty bits blurted out so it wasn't taken down. Then he did voice-over commentary about how I had tormented him during high school and that he got even with me, that he finally won against his bully.

I live with my parents. I figured since they weren't on social media so they wouldn't see it. When I went to work the next morning, I got some of the same treatment that I'd given Bruce. Worse, my boss, a deacon at my church, made up some dumbass excuse and fired me despite six years of stellar annual evaluations, no accidents, and a blemish–free job record.

I went home to find my things on the front lawn.

My boss the deacon had called my dad. Dad watched the video. When I got to the door, he stepped out and stopped me from going inside. My father then told me he had no son, I didn't live there anymore, and he never wanted to see me again. My mom was standing behind him crying. Mom didn't seem quite as upset as my dad was but she'd always deferred to him as her husband so she didn't speak up as he slammed the door in my face.

I moved my things off the grass into the back of my pickup and drove to my best friend's house. I got a slightly better reaction than I did from my folks. I told him I needed someplace to live. He said he couldn't let me stay with him in the house or people would think he was gay too but he wasn't going to let me be homeless. He had a beat–up trailer he took on vacations and said I could stay in it until I got back on my feet.

The problem is I'm so adrift I can't even see where to try to put my feet.

What should I do?

–Forced Out Of The Closet in Clayton

Dear Forced,

If one were foolish enough to believe in karma, it would seem in many ways you are only getting what you deserve for your past tormenting of your former classmate. However, if you are going to believe in something, do not waste time on karma. Instead, turn to Cthulhu.

Just because you might deserve this, does not mean you should just bend over and take it without striking back.

Your species spends too much of its time fretting and hating one another based on procreation identity variations, ignoring so many more of humanity's tremendous flaws in favor of things truly inconsequential. Everything in the universe wants to kill the lot of you yet so many humans waste their efforts hating others who use or rearrange their pelvic bits differently. No wonder you all need Cthulhu's guidance.

Bruce did an efficient job of destroying your life as you knew it. You destroyed his life in high school but tried to make amends but your kindness was used against you. Many of your kind say that two wrongs do not make a right. In this they are correct but so what? Neither do three or four or more wrongs but they can be quite entertaining to watch. Nowhere is it written that you must stop at merely a pair of wrongs. You may pile wrongs one atop the other until they collapse, killing all in the vicinity.

Stop wallowing in your misfortune and set out on a quest for vengeance.

Bruce broke the law by filming your procreation without your consent but will likely never be prosecuted in a court of law. Your country also has laws on the books regarding posting revenge pornography but it would take much for him to be charged. Fortunately, in your society, there is a more important court, that of public opinion. You can bring him to this court and ruin his life yet again.

You are lucky that Bruce was foolish enough in his quest for vengeance to put the evidence of his crime up for all to see. Quickly, before he wises up or the social media platform realizes what the video is, download or record a copy of it for yourself. To win this war, you will need to get public opinion on your side. These days the best way to do that is with a so-called heartfelt video. Simply tell the camera what you have told me. That you regretted your actions in high school. Realizing how horrible you had been, you decided to be a better person so when you bumped into the former object of your tormenting, you had to try to make amends. You explained why you did what you did, in the process coming out of the closet for the first time to your former victim. You then apologized and asked for his forgiveness. The burden weighing down your soul was lessened by Bruce offering you the very forgiveness you sought. Then he embraced you like he cared.

Knowing from your confession and because of where you had grown up you had absolutely no romantic experience, Bruce took advantage of your emotional vulnerability and seduced you. You thought you had found your first love, but it all turned out to be lies because he seduced you into having sex under false pretenses.

Bruce reveled in ripping out your heart before you had even gotten out of his bed. He had recorded your first intimate encounter and placed it online for all the world to see. You begged him not to, saying you did not consent to this. That you only trusted him enough to procreate with because he offered you forgiveness. Then Bruce betrayed you by revealing your secret and forcing you out of the closet before you were ready.

The beauty of this is it is all true. These facts will win you sympathy from a large portion of your procreation community, largely because it is backed up by Bruce's own post. Bruce did all that knowing full well that it would destroy your life, and his actions left you alone, jobless, and homeless. In your video say what city he works in, where he works, and does his employer condone his actions?

With some more well-placed social media posts and videos, you may be able to ostracize Bruce from the larger procreation community that you both belong to because while they will likely be able to relate to being bullied for who they are, they will be far more sympathetic to you having had your life destroyed by Bruce revealing your sexual orientation to the world at large without your consent and before you were ready. You may even generate enough bad publicity that his employer publicly announces that his actions do not align with their philosophy so they have fired him.

Do not think that *your* former employer should get off scot-free. You will need to engage that most feared of the human species–a lawyer. Many will work on contingencies while others will work pro bono in service of a cause. Sue your former employer for wrongful termination based on sexual orientation. The fines for this can be hefty and to avoid that, the bad publicity, and the possible financial penalty of a successful lawsuit by you against them, they may offer you a large amount of money to make the whole thing go away. You will have to decide if you prefer money or vengeance. While extra vengeance would be more fun, money is more practical. It does not appear as though you will have much of a social life in your hometown so you can use that money to finance relocating to a place more accepting of your procreational leanings. If you have enough money left, consider suing Bruce–your lawyer will likely be able to tell you for what and then you can make him pay even more. One thing all humans should learn from magnificent Cthulhu is that one should never be ashamed of what and who they are, even if it is something as lowly as a human. That and if anyone tries to harm you in any way, you must destroy them utterly.

Dear Cthulhu,

It's me again, the lady who literally loves a duck. You'll be happy to know that I did go to the emergency room and had Mallard's member removed from inside of me. There was a great deal of embarrassment as well as much laughing at my expense. However, I can see now that it was the smartest thing to do.

I also took your advice about trying out men again including going to a bar at last call. I went a few towns over so I wouldn't see anyone who'd recognize me and picked up the best-looking guy still there at three in the morning. He was drunk but could still stumble to my car. He was game, so I took him home. You are right about him being willing to wear a duck mask while we made sexy time.

He wasn't Mallard, but it was less complicated and fun. The guy was so drunk his world must have been spinning because he was holding on tight and pumping like he was trying not to fall off of me. I started to scream and moan as things got good and then realized my mistake. I hadn't closed or locked my bedroom door. It turns out Mallard is a very jealous duck. He had once fought off that burglar to save me after all. When he entered my bedroom and saw the man in the duck mask on top of me, Mallard flew at his face and started pecking at the mask. The mask spun so the drunk guy couldn't see out the eye holes. He got off me, trying to get away from the feathers of fury attacking him. He ended up tripping over his own boots and smashing his head on my footboard.

I took the mask off and checked his neck like you see people do on TV. He had no pulse, so I tried mouth-to-mouth and CPR but Mallard started attacking my face. I ended up having to hide in my closet until my duck calmed down and left the room. I rushed back to the guy but by then it was too late. The guy I'd picked up at the bar was dead.

I freaked out for a bit. I thought about calling the cops but they put down bears and other animals that kill people and I didn't want them to kill Mallard, so 911 wasn't an option.

I had no idea what I should do with the body, but I still hadn't forgiven my ex–boyfriend Donald for all the pain and torture his cheating put me through. I came up with a plan. I used a bunch of extra strength cleaning wipes to wipe down the guy (I never did get his name–it hadn't seemed important at the time) including his hands, face, the inside of his mouth, and his pelvic region. He had a huge knot, but the blow hadn't made him bleed. After getting dressed, I dragged the corpse and put it in my trunk then drove and dumped the dead body in Donald's backyard.

No one must've seen me because the cops arrested my ex. The news (I'm in Duluth, Georgia, not Minnesota) says it looks like he's going to take a plea deal to avoid the death penalty.

Donald was a total rat bastard but I still feel a tad guilty. Should I send an anonymous letter to the police letting them know they have the wrong guy? I mean I don't want to go to jail but shouldn't I do something? After all, I used to think I was in love with Donald.

–Love A Duck Who Killed A Man Dressed As A Duck While We Were Making Love In Duluth

Dear Duluth,

Penning any sort of correspondence to the authorities will likely not change your ex-boyfriend's fate. District attorneys prefer a sure thing to a convoluted explanation. Worse for you, someone might be curious enough to look into what you wrote. If their investigation uncovers fingerprints or any sort of DNA and you or a family member is in a database, it could lead back to you. You could claim that as his ex-girlfriend you were trying to help but if your cleaning wipes weren't thorough enough, you could have left DNA evidence on the corpse. If they find something on their own and come after you, you might be best to present a defense that your ex was jealous and attacked the dead man after the two of you made love. And because it was a one–night stand and you never exchanged names, you had no idea that you knew the victim who had died.

Dear Cthulhu,

A bit ago, I wrote to you about how as a drunken seventeen-year-old, I stole the Olympic torch and almost burned down parts of my college.

Your advice about having my lawyer point out that the university's policies allowed me, a minor, to get very drunk on campus and by threatening to talk about it had the charges dropped within a day. The video of campus security pulling me off a phone booth and smashing my face into the sidewalk made their lawyer offer up a lot of money in exchange for keeping me quiet. She was also worried that if the story about a drunken minor being beaten by school security got too much play, enrollment would drop and they stood to lose tens of millions.

They offered me a deal. There were only three weeks left in the semester, so they would pass me in all my classes and award me a bachelor's and master's degree. Not that they were offering anything I hadn't earned. Because of the horrific torture of my parents using me as basically a slave, going home on breaks was its own special kind of hell, so I stayed at college during all the summers and breaks. To be able to stay in the dorm, I had to take classes and earned every one of those credits.

I'd been majoring in philosophy and was just dragging out my time until I was legal, so I wouldn't have to go home. Once they realized I was no longer available to be abused, my parents tried to send their Llama, Larry, to stay with me for a month while they went on a cruise to Hawaii, but my RA convinced them the University had a very strict no Llama policy.

In exchange for the degrees and a million dollars–my lawyer tried for more but because of the fire damage I caused by running naked through them while carrying the Olympic torch they wouldn't increase the amount—I had to sign a paper saying I would not sue the university, absolved them of any responsibility for my actions, not bash them in interviews or social media, and agree to never return to the campus. In addition to giving me the pair of degrees, they wouldn't press charges.

My lawyer convinced me it was the best deal I was going to get. Since I avoided going to jail, I signed the papers.

It turns out that as a minor, my parents needed to co-sign and the college—unbeknownst to me—had my parents waiting in a nearby office to sign as my guardians. If I had known they were involved, I would have held off signing for a few months until I turned eighteen.

And I would have been right to do so. The lawyer got a third of the million and he gave my parents a check for the rest as they were my guardians.

My parents didn't give me a cent and told me I was on my own, which means I'm homeless. They said they had already given my room to Llama Larry, so they didn't have the space for me anymore.

My lawyer shrugged when I said he tricked me. The university laughed because they had planned it this way, so I got nothing and had signed away my rights to do anything about it.

I snapped. I wanted to not let any of them get away with this, but what could I do? Nada except get drunk.

I woke up the next morning dressed in all-black clothes,

including a full mask and night vision goggles, none of which I recognized, but they smelled of smoke.

I checked a strange phone in my pocket and freaked out at what was on the camera roll. Apparently, I'd had a busy night. The track phone had dozens of pictures on the camera roll.

The first pictures were at my childhood home and showed my parents in various states of undress with Llama Larry doing some very nasty things.

The next set had my lawyer with his pants down, on top of a judge's bench laying over the judge's big chair with a big pile of poo under him.

The last had the college president standing in one of the science buildings holding a can of gasoline and a lit zippo lighter. I checked the college's homepage and that building had burned down during the night.

All of them were wearing sunglasses. I can only assume that was because I drugged them–I had accidentally been registered in a 300-level pharmacy class because the registrar couldn't tell the difference between Philosophy and Pharmacy, so I do have some knowledge of drugs–before placing them into these compromising positions. I guess I didn't want them to look unconscious in the pictures.

The phone had a series of texts sharing each of them their shame shots with the message *Pay me what you owe me.* Thank goodness I didn't sign them or use my regular phone.

My question is, will the cops be able to track it to me? Do you think there is a chance that none of them will report it? Drunk Me also took more pictures with them interacting in intimate ways with a watermelon, ball-peen hammer, potted plants, cottage cheese, and inflatable people and animal dolls.

My parents texted back. It seems I may have also kidnapped the llama, but I have no idea where Larry is. If I did, I might be tempted to demand a ransom.

So I'm pretty sure I did a lot of bad things to get even with everyone involved in taking my settlement money. How much time do you think I'll have to do in prison? Do you think I will get any leniency for being a minor?

–Olympic Streaker and now Drunk Freaker

Dear Streaker,

I think there is a very strong chance none of them will report any of it in order to make sure those pictures are not released on the internet. The university president could be on the hook for burning down part of his own university. The lawyer would be censored or possibly disbarred, depending on the pull of the judge whose bench he defecated on. And you could make a good case for malpractice for him not informing you about the involvement of your parents.

The wild card is your parents and just how attached they are to the llama. They might be willing to go down in flames just to take you down with them. See what you can do to locate and return Larry intact. There would be no benefit from ransom because you could hold the threat of sending the pictures of them and the llama to the authorities. Tell them you will make sure the llama is taken away because everyone will think they abused the llama. In order to keep the llama, they will likely not contact the police if they know it will hurt them as much as it hurts you.

You have made an impressive start at taking your vengeance. Do not stop until you are done. Let all involved know that you expect money from them. You know the lawyer should be able to give you his third and your parents their two-thirds. Add a significant but not unpayable amount as a penalty. See how much you can get from the university president—see if you can find out his salary and holdings before deciding. Since alcohol seems to bring out the best in you consider drinking before doing any of this.

The problem will be avoiding being caught not once but

during all three money drops. You could demand cash but that leaves you to a retaliatory killing by those you are blackmailing. To reduce this risk, put in place a system on a separate social media account so it is set up to post the pictures in the future and you have to keep resetting the posting date to keep everything from going public and let all involved know that if you are unable to change the date, it all gets posted with all of them tagged in the photos. Getting that amount of cash in person leaves you vulnerable to being robbed later because you will have difficulty depositing it into a bank. You could simply have all involved gift you the money, but that leaves you vulnerable to being charged with blackmail. Another option is to use cryptocurrency. The various types have had ups and downs and some are worthless, but you are not in it for the long haul. Simply arrange for payment and cash out immediately so any downturn in the market will not wipe out your money. You can then claim the money in a bank account and not have to hide it. Another lawyer and an accountant may be able to help you set up ways to pay fewer taxes. You can donate ten percent off the top to charity to lower your tax burden. May I suggest the non-profit Cult of Cthulhu or my personal charity, The Cthulhu Orphanage and All You Can Eat Buffet.

Dear Cthulhu,

I read the letter from *Champagne Room Romeo Who May Have Popped His Cork One Time Too Many* with interest.

I'm an exotic dancer. Honestly, the word stripper somewhat triggers me but I will tolerate strip dancer. Unlike many of my coworkers, I was trained in classical ballet, clog dancing, and polka for over a decade. I even danced professionally on the stage before a pregnant dancer's water broke during the performance, causing me to slip and tear my ACL.

The injury ended my career as a classical dancer and left me adrift in the world. I had no other skills besides dancing and I'd dropped out of high school to pursue my career starring in the Polka Bears On Ice tour, based on the cartoon that merged Shakespeare's Romeo and Juliet with the beauty of Polka as performed by anthropomorphic bears. I played Lady Goldilocks Capulet.

Oddly enough it's my pregnancy that's led to my current predicament. After my knee injury sidelined me from my career, I was left destitute. My parents wouldn't take me in. Of course, that may have been due to me telling them to shove certain things where the sun doesn't shine when they dared suggest that Polka dancing on ice skates was neither an art form nor a good long-term career choice, certainly not one promising enough to quit high school over. They even suggested I just do it over summer break. What idiots! Everyone knows ice skating tours happen in the winter to take advantage of the downtime of ice hockey rinks.

In retrospect, they were right but I'm not about to tell those know-it-alls.

As a seasonal employee, I didn't qualify for unemployment and apparently, I'd signed a contract stating that I was an independent contractor instead of an employee which meant I didn't get workers comp for the injury.

I had to volunteer to let some strange doctor guy operate on me as the only way I could afford to get medical care, although, for some strange reason, he called it surgerizing. Other than an infection that caused my knee to swell up to three times its normal size for a few months, the surgery turned out okay.

As we ice dancers lived in trailers that followed the show, I was left homeless when I got fired for getting hurt. The doctor let me stay in his garage clinic for a couple of days after the surgerizing. I offered to entertain his patients with interpretive clog dancing while they were in his waiting room in exchange for a place to live and food. He kicked me out and I had no place to go.

As I wandered the streets looking for a place to sleep, I saw a flyer on a lamppost that said *Dancers Wanted* and listed an address for auditions. I was thrilled but not sure if my knee would hold up. I needn't have worried as they were being held in a strip club. I may have been homeschooled up until ninth grade but even I realized this wasn't the kind of dancing job I was looking for.

I didn't have any other options, so I got up on stage and asked them what kind of routine they wanted me to do. They told me just to take off my shirt and bra and jump up and down. I was hired on the spot.

On the plus side, I get to choreograph my own routines.

Some of the other girls even paid me to choreograph theirs. I geared my moves to take the pressure off my knee because even after the surgerizing, it still buckled from time to time. And oddly enough beep at 6 AM each morning. I think he may have left a watch of something in there during the operation.

The most comfortable position for me was sitting down, so I found myself leaning toward giving out lap dances. There is a large group of patrons at the club who come in sweatpants so they can feel the dancers' accordion playing the polka better. It grossed out the other girls who avoid these guys whenever they can. I wasn't crazy about it, but years of dance training gave me such control over my lower body movements that it doesn't take long to give these sweaties what they are really there for. Like Honeyshaker, I found that a few encouraging noises, doe eyes, and a huge smile at the end led to huge tips. I even instituted a fifty percent sweatpants surcharge and because of my skill set, most of the sweaties paid without balking. To cut a long, disgusting story involving many poor life choices short, I ended up specializing in lap dances. A few sweaties didn't like the surcharge and under-tipped, so I cut them off for a few weeks. They complained to management who told me I couldn't pick and choose who I saw.

I disagreed as the club made me sign an independent contract agreement. Fool me once, shame on me. Twice ain't happening. I pointed out that by IRS regs they can't tell an independent contractor what clients to see and if they did, then I was an employee and needed workers comp and benefits like health insurance, paid days off, vacation time, and so on. They said no way. I countered by mentioning that I wondered what might happen if someone called the IRS about this issue. Strip clubs deal in large amounts of cash and I suspected they didn't want their returns looked at too closely. Since they took a cut of each lap dance, I was their biggest earner, so when all was said and done they decided to back my bans.

Exotic dancing is not without its risks. One night this guy lurked in the parking lot until I left to go home and jumped me with a knife for banning him. The bouncers rushed to help me but I didn't need them. I was still wearing my clogs and my legs are ridiculously strong–ask a gym rat to stand on his toes and we'll see who needs leg day. Plus, I can do full splits, so clog kicking this creeper under his chin, even with my bad knee, was no problem. I broke his jaw and the creeper hit the pavement where I proceeded to do a rather stompy routine on his groin which was only protected by sweatpants.

The creeper curled up in a ball until the cops came. The bouncers backed me up that he attacked me, so once he got out of the hospital he took a plea deal and went to jail.

After the local news coverage and the security footage of me defending myself, my popularity soared for a month. My "crotch stomp" even became a Klik Klok dance trend.

All was well until I came home after going to the gym one day and bumped into the mailman on my porch holding a package I'd ordered. Although it was weird that he wasn't wearing a postal uniform, although it was the right colors and could pass for the uniform from a distance. He said it was casual Friday. It was also odd that he was taking the package away from my door.

Postal was cute. Like really cute and I hadn't nailed anyone in months. I had a couple of guys in the ice show I'd bang when I got thirsty, sometimes while we skated after hours. Trust me you've never really experienced a good banging until you've done it on ice skates at 25MPH. I had no desire to bonk any of the patrons, especially the sweaties. The bouncers were hot but a bit clingy and some of the other dancers were doing them on the side and I didn't need the drama.

I figured Postal would be perfect for a good banging and I was right. He delivered his package with care, although when he left he tried to take my package with him.

A month later, I was riding the porcelain pony like a drunk rodeo clown with salmonella. It didn't go away. I even puked on a sweaty but he tipped me extra. It didn't take long for me to realize I was knocked up.

I waited outside to talk to Postal when he delivered my mail but it turns out my mail carrier is a woman. She said she was working the day Postal delivered. I called the Post Office to see if it was some special delivery guy. It wasn't. Turns out they've been having a rash of packages ripped off by porch pirates and that Postal was most likely there to steal my package.

With the real father out of the financial support picture, I was in trouble. I'm keeping my baby. When I left my parents told me they wished they'd unalived me before I was born and I've never been so hurt. One of the reasons I was so mean back to them. I wasn't doing that to my kid.

I suspect a chunk of my customer base will be put off once my belly starts bulging. What if I don't look hot after I give birth? My earning power will plummet. I've been freaking out, worried I'd end up homeless again, but this time with a kid. Then I read Romeo's letter and was inspired. I could tell each of my regular sweaties that I was pregnant and that it was one of them. I looked it up and a basic paternity test can cost a hundred bucks but a legal one runs about two grand. A lawyer charges a couple hundred an hour and a paternity lawsuit would run lots of hours.

I traded a private lap dance to a lawyer patron in his house so his wife could watch in exchange for him writing up a contract. It says that in exchange for a one-time fee of five grand, I waived any claims of paternity in perpetuity against the signer. Five grand is a lot cheaper than them paying for the costs of defending against me suing for paternity. I figure I'll take home almost two years' salary. And if we have to take one to court, I have no problem with that. I'll lose but it will show the others I'm serious and hopefully convince them to pay up. My lawyer agreed to be paid in lap dances. Turns out he and his wife had their best naughty time in years after my last visit.

Am I missing anything?

–Dancer Doing Laps In St. Paul

Dear Laps,

It is a good plan. Most men will be more willing to make a relatively small one-time payment rather than risk almost two decades of child support. It seems likely most will pay rather than lay out more money to fight you in court, especially as some of them may be involved in relationships. It has been Cthulhu's experience that few things put a damper on so-called romantic relationships than another woman claiming one's man fathered their child.

Some of these sweaties may have had vasectomies, so I would advise letting them off the hook as pursuing matters could upend your plans. Taking multiple men to court unsuccessfully, especially if you happen to get the same judge, will be held against you.

One thing to consider is that by doing this you are effectively ending your ability to work at this club. The management may be upset that you are effectively blackmailing their clients, which, if word spreads, will decrease their business. Also since much of your regular livelihood depends on catering to these sweaties, have you considered the effect this will have on your financial bottom line? Yes, you will have the finances to pursue other means of earning a living but do you think these sweaties will still take advantage of your services after finding out you allegedly became pregnant by giving a lap dance? Your skill set may be good but as you said, fool them once shame on you. Do you think they will be fooled again? Only the very desperate or the truly stupid would. While their numbers are higher than one might believe, it will not be enough to make a living off.

You could cater to a new niche of clientele as there are men who would pay extra to get a lap dance from a pregnant woman or you can take the time up until giving birth to explore other options for gainful employment. There are many options available and your local unemployment office may have some options available even if as an independent contractor you do not qualify for unemployment payments.

Should that fail and your physique holds up enough to still be able to evoke desire in the male of your species, use some of the money to relocate to a new area so you can continue to fill your exotic dancing niche in a new community. Use a new stage name as well.

However, you have given up too easily on making the genetic provider of your pending offspring pay. You think you won't be able to find him, but you may be mistaken. Contact your local police department and inquire if they have made any arrests for similar porch pirate crimes. If they have, request to view the perpetrators' mug shots. You may find the man. If he is free, you can take him to court, get a positive paternity test, and get court-ordered child support. If he has been imprisoned, it may be more difficult, but he likely has parents. Perhaps they are in a better financial position. While you cannot force them to give you money, they may wish to help out with their grandchild. And perhaps you may be fortunate and find a better family environment than the one you grew up in.

Have A Dark Day.

There has long been a debate among certain obscure and drunken literary scholars about whether **PATRICK THOMAS** was raised by Cthulhu, a leprechaun in a Manhattan bar, or two human parents. What there is no arguing about is that Patrick is the award-winning author of 40 books including the beloved fantasy humor *Murphy's Lore series* (9 books from *Tales from Bulfinche's Pub* to *The Mug Life*), as well as 2 books in the future space adventures in the *Startenders* series.

The Murphy's Lore After Hours spin-offs star the half pixie/ogre Terrorbelle (*Fairy With A Gun, Fairy Rides The Lightning,* and *Terrorbelle The Unconquered*); the former demon-possessed serial killer Agent Karver of the Department of Mystic Affairs (*Dead To Rites, Rites of Passage*); the cursed magí Hex (*By Darkness Cursed* and *By Invocation Only*); Vince Argus, the Soul For Hire (*Greatest Hits*); and Negral, a forgotten Sumerian god who works as Hell's Detective (*Lore & Dysorder, Bullets & Brimstone,* and the graphic novel *The Moon Maniac* with Blair Webb).

His *Mystic Investigators* paranormal mystery series includes *Shadows & Brimstone* (omnibus of *Bullets & Brimstone* and *From The Shadows* with John L. French), *Once Upon In Crime* (omnibus of *Once More Upon A Time* and *Partners In Crime* with Diane Raetz) *Mystic Investigators,* and *Mean Streets. Assassins' Ball* is his first traditional mystery, co-written with John L. French. He co-edited *Camelot 13, New Blood, Hear Them Roar* and was an editor for the magazines *Fantastic Stories of the Imagination* and *Pirate Writings*.

His other works include the steampunk *As The Gears Turn.* the space epic *Exile & Entrance,* and the *Bikini Jones* series. Patrick's darkly humorous advice column *Dear Cthulhu* has been running since 2005 and has 6 collections including *Cthulhu Knows Best* and *What Would Cthulhu Do?* The Dear Cthulhu advice empire has expanded from magazines and books to radio as Dear Cthulhu now broadcasts monthly on the show Destinies: The Voice of Science Fiction which is hosted by Dr. Howard Margolin.

Over 100 of his stories have been published in magazines and anthologies. His noir novella appears in *Murder in Montague Falls.* A number of his books were part of the props department of the *CSI* television show and *Nightcaps* was even thrown at a suspect's head. His urban fantasy *Fairy With A Gun* had been optioned for film and TV by Laurence Fishburne's Cinema Gypsy Productions. Top Men Productions has turned his *Soul For Hire* Story, *Act of Contrition,* into a short film.

He writes books for kids as PATRICK T. FIBBS including the YA *Emotional Support Nightmare,* the midde readers *Undead Kid Diaries: Over My Dead Body,* the Babe B. Bear Mysteries: *Bad Hair Day, Joy Reaper Checks Out,* the picture book *Fushcia The Mermaid Who Loved Pink,* and *the Ughabooz* picture books *5 Silly Monsters Jumping On The Zed* and *On Top Of A Yeti,* and the early reader *Soggy Goes to the Beach.*

Please drop by www.patthomas.net or follow him at I_PatrickThomas at Twitter or www.facebook.com/PatrickThomasAuthor to learn more.

BIKINI JONES

**Being *CURSED* to wear a bikini
Won't stop this Hero
From *SAVING* the world**

Dear Cthulhu

**THE ADVICE
COLUMN TO
END ALL
ADVICE COLUMNS**

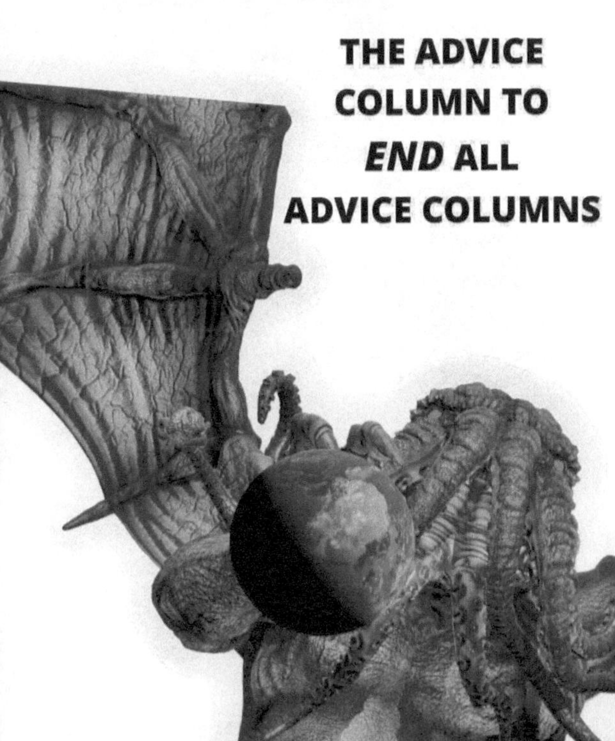

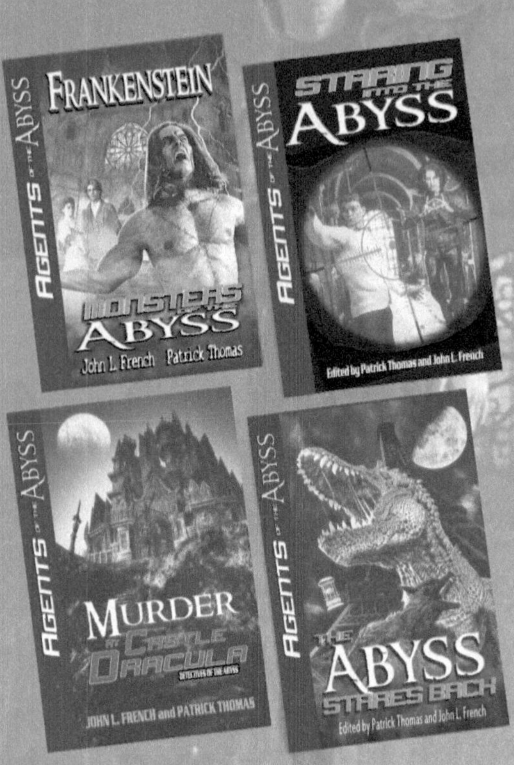

The Past, Present, and Future of the Abyss!

The Inspirations for the
Rising Storm: The Starborne card game

Features all
6 books in the series in
one deluxe volume!

NO TEACHERS. NO PARENTS SCHOOL IS OUT.... OF THIS WORLD

www.talehaven.com

EVEN THE TEENAGE QUEEN OF DARKNESS NEEDS A FRIEND